ABOUT THIS BOOK

EINSTEIN ANDERSON Goes to Bat
Seymour Simon
Illustrated by Fred Winkowski

Is a genuine, bloodthirsty vampire on the loose in the town
of Sparta? Why can't the superfast baseball bat hit a slow
curve? Sixth-grader Einstein Anderson, baseball freak and
lover of bad puns, uses his incredible scientific knowledge
to unravel the clues to ten baffling—and entertaining—
mysteries.

"Related with spirt and peppered with puns, this series will
intrigue science buffs."
—ALA *Booklist*

"Entertaining"
—*School Library Journal*

ALSO IN THIS SERIES

Seymour Simon (signature)

EINSTEIN ANDERSON

Goes to Bat

Seymour Simon

Illustrated by Fred Winkowski

Puffin Books

For my nieces and nephews:
Debbie, David, Bryan, Alexander, Dena

PUFFIN BOOKS
Viking Penguin Inc., 40 West 23rd Street, New York, New York 10010, U.S.A.
Penguin Books Ltd, Harmondsworth, Middlesex, England
Penguin Books Australia Ltd, Ringwood, Victoria, Australia
Penguin Books Canada Limited, 2801 John Street, Markham, Ontario, Canada L3R 1B4
Penguin Books (N.Z.) Ltd, 182–190 Wairau Road, Auckland 10, New Zealand

First published by The Viking Press 1982
Published in Puffin Books 1987
Text copyright © Seymour Simon, 1982
Illustrations copyright © Viking Penguin Inc., 1982
All rights reserved
Printed in the United States of America by R. R. Donnelley & Sons Company,
Harrisonburg, Virginia
Set in Trump

Library of Congress catalog card number: 86-40362
(CIP data available)
ISBN 0-14-032303-1

Contents

In this book Einstein Anderson solves puzzles by using his knowledge in these areas of science:

anatomy
technology
physics
acrobatics
zoology
meteorology
biology

Einstein Anderson Goes to Bat

1
The Vampire

Einstein Anderson couldn't believe his ears. Making a movie about a vampire was one thing, but actually having a vampire in town was quite another.

"Mom, you know that vampires do exist," Einstein said. "They live in tropical countries from Mexico south to Brazil. But they are really bats, not people who turn into bats when the sun goes down."

"Do the vampire bats drink blood?" Mrs. Anderson asked, shuddering slightly.

"Sure," Einstein said cheerfully. "The vampires feed on the blood of animals, including humans.

They have razor-sharp teeth that they use to slice into blood vessels. A vampire bat doesn't suck the blood—it laps the blood up with its tongue. You see, the vampire—"

"Never mind the details, Einstein," Mrs. Anderson interrupted. "Something funny is going on in Sparta, and I want to write a story about it for the paper before the news services send reporters here." Mrs. Anderson was a reporter and editor for the Sparta *Tribune*, one of the town's two newspapers.

Einstein's real name was Adam. He had been interested in science even before he started school. By the time he was in second grade, Adam knew so much science that his teacher began to call him Einstein, after the most famous scientist of the twentieth century. Soon all his friends began to call him Einstein. Now that Adam was in the sixth grade, even his mother and father sometimes called him Einstein.

Einstein looked thoughtfully at his mother. His glasses slipped down over his nose, and he pushed them back with his finger. "Are you sure it's not a publicity stunt for the vampire movie they're filming in the old Carlyle house at the edge of town?"

"That's what I thought," admitted Mrs. Anderson. "But one of the cameramen filming the movie, *Wings of Darkness*, came to the police chief with a weird story."

"What did he tell the chief, Mom?"

"The chief won't say. But the cameraman just called me on the phone," Mrs. Anderson said. "His name is Boris Vlad. And he says he saw a real vampire during the filming of *Wings of Darkness*. He sounded very frightened when he spoke to me over the phone. Anyway, he's coming over to my office in an hour. I'd like you to be there when he comes and listen to what he has to say."

"As the vampire said to his dentist, fangs very much," Einstein said with a grin. "I'll be happy to hear a story about a real sucker. Get it, Mom?"

Mrs. Anderson smiled and shook her head. "Let's go down to my office without any more bad jokes," she said affectionately.

Boris Vlad was a tall thin man with black hair and pale white skin. Einstein half expected to see fangs when Vlad opened his mouth. But Vlad's teeth were ordinary looking, more ordinary than his story.

"I'm an assistant cameraman on the film crew working on *Wings of Darkness*." Vlad began his story after sitting down in Mrs. Anderson's office at the *Tribune*. "It's my job to see that the lighting is set up properly before filming begins. The lighting equipment is very large and needs a heavy power line. That old mansion where most of the filming is taking place doesn't have enough electric lines, so the lines are brought in from a generator that we keep outside."

Vlad ran his fingers through his hair and shook his head. "This sounds so crazy—almost like it's part of the movie." He coughed nervously.

"Do you want a glass of water?" Mrs. Anderson asked.

"No, thanks," Vlad said. He cleared his throat. "We were filming in the afternoon. It began to get dark and we needed more lighting, so Mr. Freed, the director, said that we would take a break for supper and continue filming at eight o'clock that night."

Vlad paused again and looked down at his clenched hands. "Anyway, I was supposed to set up the lighting for the evening filming. I was standing in the room, thinking about what to do, when I heard a squeaking noise in the hall outside.

"I opened the door a crack and looked out in the hall. It was pretty dark, but I could see someone pushing a table on wheels down the hall. The table had four large jugs on it. You know, the kind that hold a gallon of cider or juice."

"Did you recognize the person wheeling the table?" asked Mrs. Anderson.

"No," Vlad said. "It was too dark. I also noticed some other things on the table—tubes and things like that. I was curious about what was happening,

but I thought it must be just some person taking away some empty bottles from supper.

"I decided not to bother with what I saw and began to set up the lighting. I was busy working when I began to hear another sound. This time it was a kind of crying. The sound really frightened me. I went out into the hall to see what it was. I saw a light in the room at the end of the hall, and I walked over quietly. Inside the room I saw this shadowy figure bending over a body on the bed. The figure was using the tubes to fill the bottles with blood. It was horrible. He had already filled two bottles and was just starting to fill the third bottle."

"What did you do?" Mrs. Anderson asked.

"I yelled and ran toward the figure. But I slipped on the rug and fell on the floor. I hit my head and must have conked out for a while. When I came to, the figure was gone."

"What about the body on the bed?" Einstein asked.

"It turned out to be Christine Farrar, the assistant director. She was pretty woozy and didn't remember anything. But she had these two little marks on her neck."

"Did she see a doctor?" Einstein asked.

"No, she said she was O.K. and just took the next few days off."

"Was anyone else bothered by the shadowy figure?" Einstein asked.

"No," Vlad said. "Christine was the only one bothered."

"Say, Mr. Vlad," Einstein said, "do you act in the movie as well as do the lighting?"

Vlad looked at Einstein and smiled slightly. "Yes," he said. "Why do you ask?"

"Because you gave such a good performance just now," Einstein said. "But I'm afraid your story just doesn't hold water, or perhaps I should say blood."

Can you solve the puzzle: How does Einstein know that Vlad is not telling the truth?

"You may not believe my story, but how can you prove it's not true?" Vlad asked Einstein.

"You said that the shadowy figure you saw was wheeling a table with four empty gallon jugs. Then you said that the figure had filled two of the jugs with the blood of the assistant director."

"Are you saying assistant directors don't have blood?" laughed Vlad.

"Not two gallons of blood," Einstein said. "Few people have that much blood. The average adult human has about ten to twelve pints—about one and a half gallons. And you said no one else had been bothered by the vampire. So where did all that blood come from?"

Vlad shook his head ruefully. "I knew the story wasn't going to be believed. But Mr. Freed and Christine Farrar thought it would be a good publicity stunt for the movie. They said I'd get a bigger part if I could convince the newspapers that it really happened."

"I think you should tell the chief of police that your story was just a publicity stunt," Mrs. Anderson said.

"O.K.," said Vlad. "But you have to admit I put on a good performance." Vlad got up and shook hands with Einstein. "I can see why you're called Einstein," he said. "See you around."

After Vlad had left, Einstein turned to his mother and said, "I just remembered something else about vampires."

"What's that?" Mrs. Anderson asked.

"Just that they can't play baseball in the afternoon. Their bats don't come out till after dark."

2
The Anti-Gravity Machine

It was the Saturday after Einstein had discovered the secret of the "vampire." Einstein was having a catch with Margaret Michaels in the backyard of her house. Soon they would eat lunch, and then Margaret was going to show Einstein her strange discovery.

Margaret was Einstein's classmate, good friend, and arch rival. She was about as tall as Einstein and good at sports. Both of them were on the sixth grade softball team. Both were also good students.

Science was Margaret's favorite subject, too. Margaret and Einstein often worked with each other on experiments after school and on weekends. They enjoyed talking about important subjects such as telescope making, weather prediction, space travel, and who would get the best mark on the next sixth grade science test.

"Do you want to eat lunch now, Einstein?" Margaret asked. "We can have peanut butter and jelly sandwiches and make a salad out of some of the garden vegetables."

"Sounds great," Einstein responded. "If we have lunch out here, can we call it The Garden of Eatin?"

Margaret laughed. "Then we'd need a serpent," she said. "Maybe my pet garter snake Sylvester will do. But the apples aren't ripe yet. Anyway, let's go and make lunch."

Eating a picnic lunch was fun, and the food was delicious. After lunch they cleaned up and went back into Margaret's house. Margaret led the way up a folding ladder into the attic. The attic was hot and dusty. Old trunks and furniture filled the room.

"Some of the things up here must be a hundred years old," Einstein said, looking around.

"I think some are even older than that," Margaret replied. "The house was built in the middle of the last century. It's been remodeled since then, but some of the furniture in the attic belonged to the

original owners. No one has opened the trunks in years. I had to oil the hinges just to open the lids.''

"Did you find anything inside the trunks?" Einstein asked.

"Mostly old clothes, magazines, and books," Margaret said. "It was fun looking at advertisements in magazines that date back to the 1930s. But I found something more interesting than old magazines in one of the trunks."

"What was that?"

"I found a letter written during World War Two. The owner of the house at that time, Mr. Pecksniff, was an inventor. The letter tells about an invention he was working on, maybe for the government."

"What kind of invention?"

"I want you to see for yourself," Margaret replied. "Here's the letter. It's dated January 1943." Margaret handed a soiled envelope to Einstein.

Einstein took the letter and turned it over. "There's no address and no stamp," he said.

"I think Mr. Pecksniff got sick about that time and never got around to mailing the letter," Margaret said. "But the letter itself is very interesting."

Einstein unfolded the letter and began to read.

Dear Mr. President:

My anti-gravity machine finally works. It is a great day for the Allied Powers. I have taken a Polaroid photo of my X-3 machine hovering in the air to prove to the world that I am not mad after all. I will hide the machine and the plans for building it until you can send a committee of scientists to

*investigate. Please send them quickly be-
cause I am ill and do not have long to live.*

The letter was signed, "Mr. Pecksniff."

"Do you expect me to believe this, Margaret?"
Einstein asked. "I think you made up the whole
thing. I never heard of an anti-gravity machine, and I
don't think it's possible to invent one, either."

"Maybe you'll believe it when you see this." Margaret held out a photograph to Einstein. "I found this
in the letter."

Einstein took the photograph and examined it care-
fully. It was a bit blurry, but it seemed to show a
strange-looking machine in midair between the
ground and the branch of a tree overhead. The back of
the photo was dated January 1943.

"What do you think of that photo?" Margaret asked
dramatically. "It proves that Pecksniff must have
invented the machine he writes about. For all I know,
that anti-gravity machine might be hidden someplace
in this attic. If you help me clean up the attic, maybe
we can find it or at least find the plans to build
another machine."

Einstein pushed back his glasses, which were slip-
ping down. "So *that's* what this letter is all about," he
said. "I think the only real invention here is the letter
itself. And the only thing it does is to get me to help
you clean the attic."

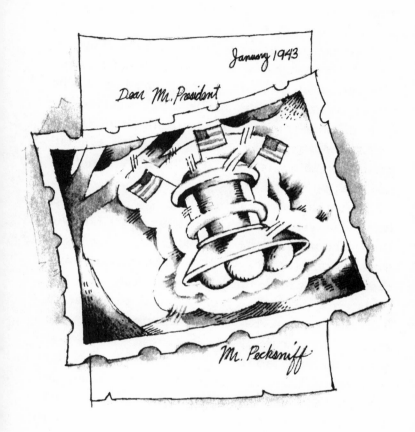

Can you solve the puzzle: How does Einstein know the letter is an invention?

"What do you mean by that?" Margaret asked innocently. "How can you doubt what you see in the photo?"

"You must have taken that yourself," Einstein replied. "You probably tied a black thread to some contraption you made and hung it from a branch. The thread would be invisible against a dark background."

"But how do you know that I took the photograph?" persisted Margaret. "There's no way you can tell when the photo was taken. Maybe Mr. Pecksniff did take the photo back in 1943."

"He would have had a difficult time taking a Polaroid snapshot in 1943," Einstein said. "Dr. Edwin Land, who invented the Polaroid camera, first began working on the idea in 1943. The first Polaroid camera wasn't made until 1947, four years later."

Margaret shook her head. "Too bad. I thought I'd fool you this time. But you'll help me clean up the attic anyway, won't you? There really are lots of interesting things to see."

"I hope all those interesting things don't make me *see*-sick," Einstein said.

"Einstein!" Margaret exclaimed. "It's those jokes that are going to make *me* sick."

"Well, as the mountain said to the volcano after the earthquake, it's not my fault."

3
The Batty Invention

"I've become interested in inventing better sports equipment," Stanley said. "There's a lot of science involved in sports, and let's face it: who knows more about science than I do?"

"I don't think I have time enough to answer that question," Einstein replied with a smile. "My mom expects me home for supper before next year."

"Ha, ha, very funny," Stanley said without smiling in return. "Listen, Einstein. A person can make a lot of money inventing a new kind of sneaker or a better football helmet. Can you imagine a baseball glove that sticks to a ball, or a radio-controlled basketball that always goes through the hoop?"

"Those are great ideas," commented Einstein. "But how would a baseball player be able to throw the ball to a teammate if his glove sticks to the ball? And it might get pretty boring playing with a radio-controlled basketball when each player never misses."

Stanley brushed back his long black hair, which was falling into his eyes. "Well, maybe there would be a few minor problems with those inventions," he conceded. "But those are just examples of what I might do in the future."

He paused and then dramatically announced, "My new invention will revolutionize baseball. I'll become as famous as Abner Doubleday, baseball's inventor. Who knows? My home town of Sparta might even build a science museum named after me."

"Your lab looks like a museum *now*," Einstein said. "A museum of wild and crazy things." He looked around Stanley's "laboratory"—an attic room that Stanley's parents let him use for his experiments. The room was overflowing with half-finished, weird-looking machines. It looked like a mad scientist's junk shop. Of course Stanley claimed that everything in the room was an important piece of scientific apparatus.

Stanley Roberts was in high school. He liked science, inventing, experimenting, and trying out new gadgets. Stanley enjoyed showing his new inventions to Einstein. Einstein liked Stanley but was always kidding him about his mistakes.

"You may make fun of my lab now," Stanley said, "but I would advise you to pay attention to my new baseball invention."

"I've already gotten some good advice from the manager of the sixth grade baseball team," Einstein replied. "She said that if at first you don't succeed, try playing second base."

"Ugh." Stanley groaned. "You're always making such awful jokes when you should be listening to me."

"Sorry about that, Stanley," Einstein apologized. "Please show me your new invention."

"I can't actually show it to you, Einstein," Stanley said. "I've just drawn up the plans, and I'm going to send them to a metal-working plant so they can construct a model of this new kind of baseball bat. But I can tell you about the bat if you give me a chance to talk without interrupting.

"I read an article in a science magazine about a new kind of metal that is very light but very tough and springy. I decided to draw up plans to make a baseball bat from that metal. The bat will be hol-

low and weigh only two ounces. Can you imagine
how fast you could swing a bat that light? And how
far you could hit a baseball with a bat like that?"

Einstein pushed back his glasses with one finger
and thought for a minute. "Sorry, Stanley," he said,

"but your bat would be better as a flyswatter than a fly ball hitter."

Can you solve the puzzle: What's wrong with Stanley's idea for a new kind of baseball bat?

"But how do you know that my bat isn't any good without even trying it?" Stanley asked.

"Because of Isaac Newton and his Laws of Motion," Einstein said. "Newton's Second Law says that the force acting on an object is equal to its mass or weight multiplied by its speed."

"That only proves that my invention will work," Stanley said. "The bat is so light that you can move it with great speed and get more force behind your swing."

"But your bat is hitting a baseball. And a baseball weighs five ounces, more than twice as much as your bat. Newton's Third Law says that for every action there is an equal and opposite reaction. So when your bat hits the ball, the bat will bounce back much more than the ball. The ball will probably knock the bat out of the batter's hands."

"I guess I'll have to junk my bat plans," Stanley said dejectedly.

"Your ideas aren't all bad," Einstein replied. "Maybe we can figure out a way to add enough weights in the right places to give your bat the maximum force with the least amount of effort."

"I'd like that," Stanley said. "Then both our names may become as well known as Abner Doubleday's."

"I know of a famous Greek who knew about

baseball two thousand years before Doubleday,"
Einstein said.

"Who was that?" Stanley asked.

"Homer," replied Einstein.

4
Paper Tiger

Einstein was standing on the lunch line in the school cafeteria when Pat Burns came up behind him. Pat Burns was the biggest bully in the sixth grade. Pat picked on all the kids in the class, but especially the smaller ones. Most of the kids called him Pat the Brat—but not to his face. He was too big and mean to risk that.

Pat tapped Einstein on the shoulder. "I wonder if I could talk to you for a minute, Einstein," he said politely.

Einstein looked at Pat with surprise. Pat usually didn't talk to anyone except to bully him in one way or another. And Pat certainly was never polite. What was going on here? Einstein wondered.

"What would you like to talk about?" Einstein asked cautiously.

"Well, you're a pretty smart kid," Pat said. "You know a lot about science and stuff like that. And sometimes you can even figure out how to beat someone who's stronger than you are. Like me, for instance."

Einstein pushed back his glasses. Then he scratched his head in bewilderment. "I don't get it. You want me to beat you at something?" he asked.

"No, no," Pat said. "You don't understand. I don't want you to beat *me* at anything. I want you to help me beat Tiger Martin."

"Tiger Martin!" Einstein exclaimed. "You want *me* to help *you* beat Tiger Martin, the eighth grade terror? He's the biggest kid in the school. He's twice as big as both of us put together. Why don't you ask your friend Herman to help you? He's bigger than I am."

"Herman can't help me against Tiger Martin," Pat said sadly. "It's just going to be Tiger against me, one to one. And the loser has to carry the winner's books around school for the rest of the year. Can you imagine *me* carrying someone else's books around!?"

"*You* shouldn't be afraid of hard work," Einstein said. "You've been fighting it successfully for years."

"If that's a joke, Einstein, I don't think it's very funny. Tiger Martin is no laughing matter." Pat paused and looked around him. "Please help me?" he asked in a low voice.

Einstein shook his head. If Pat Burns was saying "please," he must be really worried—even scared.

"O.K., Pat," Einstein agreed. "Tell me what happened and how I can help you."

"I don't want anyone else to hear the story," Pat said. "Wait till we sit down."

The boys got their lunches and took them over to a table in the rear of the cafeteria. Einstein was about to take a bite out of his tuna fish sandwich when Pat caught his arm.

"Listen to this," Pat said.

"I'd like to listen and eat at the same time, if that's all right with you," Einstein said.

"Sure, pal. Anything you do is A-O.K. with me." Pat tried to smile, but he looked upset.

"Just tell me the story," Einstein said. The idea of Pat acting like a nice guy was a bit difficult to grasp.

"I was talking to some of the fifth grade kids in the school yard this morning," Pat began, "when

Tiger Martin happened to overhear what I was saying. He came over and started to act like a big shot and—"

"What were you saying to the fifth graders?"

Pat looked uncomfortable. "I guess I was telling them that I was the strongest kid in school," he mumbled.

"Tiger Martin must have loved hearing you say that," Einstein said. "Especially since he's the strongest."

"Yeah," Pat agreed. "That's what he said. He also sort of grabbed me around the neck and asked if I'd like to have a contest with him to see who was stronger."

"Why didn't you say no?" Einstein asked.

"I couldn't say anything!" Pat exclaimed. "I could hardly breathe. Anyway, Tiger said I could choose any contest of strength I wanted. And that he'd meet me in the school yard after school." Pat paused. "Do you think you can help me beat Tiger?" he asked hopefully.

Einstein pushed back his glasses and thought for a minute. Maybe he should just let Pat get what he deserved. But Pat had said "please" and asked for help. Besides, this was a good opportunity to show Pat that using your brain was a good idea.

"Suppose you give Tiger a choice of two different tests of strength," Einstein said. "Then ask him to choose either one and you'll take the other. If he chooses the more difficult test, then you can beat him."

"But why would anyone pick a more difficult one?" Pat asked.

"He will if he thinks it's easier," Einstein replied.

"Here's what you can do. Offer Tiger this choice: He either has to fold a sheet of newspaper in half nine times or push a drinking straw through a raw potato."

"What?" Pat yelled. "That's crazy. Anyone can fold a newspaper in half nine times. And a straw would just bend if you tried to push it through a raw potato. Tiger will never fall for the trick. Some help you are!"

Einstein laughed. "Let me explain how you can win," he said.

Can you solve the puzzle: How can Pat beat Tiger?

"Go ahead and explain," Pat said gloomily. "But I don't think it will help."

"If Tiger makes the same choice that you just did, then you can't lose," Einstein said. "Folding a sheet of newspaper in half nine times sounds as if it should be easy, but it's actually impossible."

"Huh?"

"Let me explain. You see, no matter how thin or large the sheet of newspaper is to begin with, few people can fold it in half more than seven times. Each time you fold the paper you double the number of layers. By the time you get to the eighth fold, you have two hundred and fifty-six layers of paper. That's as thick as a big book. Try it."

"But even if Tiger can't fold the newspaper, I still won't win," Pat complained. "No one can push a straw through a raw potato. The straw will just bend."

"Not if you pinch one end tight with your fingers," Einstein explained. "That will trap the air inside and stiffen the straw. Use as much force as you can and strike the potato quickly. Be sure the straw goes straight into the potato, not at an angle. Practice before you try it this afternoon."

"Thanks, Einstein. I knew we'd come up with a way to beat Tiger," Pat said. "You just can't beat us brainy kids."

Pat stood up and motioned to a fifth grader eating at a nearby table. "Hey, weakling," he said. "Go get my friend Einstein a glass of water and make it fast."

Pat turned and walked away, "accidentally" knocking over someone's lunch tray.

Einstein shook his head. Pat had been nice for a while, but it looked as if he'd just had a relapse.

5
Balancing Act

Einstein was in his room reading a book about snakes when he heard his brother Dennis shout from his next-door bedroom. Dennis was eight years old and in the fourth grade. He often asked Einstein such interesting questions as why was the sky blue and would Einstein buy him an ice cream soda.

Einstein closed the book and went into Dennis's room to see what the noise was all about. Dennis was hopping around on one foot and holding his other foot with both hands. What looked like a wooden sword was lying on the floor. Dennis was also making noises that sounded like, "Ow, ooch, ow, ooch."

"Is that the latest disco dance you're doing, Dennis?" Einstein asked with a smile. "No, I guess not. It must be a rain dance."

"There's nothing funny about being hit on the toes with a sword," Dennis said.

"I know a sword can be used for *duel* purposes," Einstein said. "But just what purpose do you have in mind for the sword?"

"I have to balance the sword on end for two minutes," Dennis said.

"That makes sense," Einstein said. "But would you mind explaining a bit further?"

"It's all because of my friend Chuck. Or rather

my *ex*-friend Chuck. He bet Jane all my baseball cards that I could balance her sword for five minutes, and she said I couldn't do it even for two minutes. So I have to win that bet."

"Why does Jane have a sword?" Einstein asked. "And who is Jane, anyway?"

"Jane is a girl in my class," Dennis replied. "She's always showing off with magic tricks, juggling, and stuff like that. She was doing one of her acts in front of the class and she was about to balance a sword on her fingers. Chuck said anyone could do that, even me. Before I could say anything, Chuck had bet all my baseball cards against Jane's that I could balance the sword."

"Chuck seems to have more confidence in you than he has in himself," Einstein said.

"That's not it," Dennis said. "Chuck would just rather have me lose my cards than have him lose *his* cards."

"How did it go?" Einstein asked. "Were you able to balance the sword?"

"I didn't even get a chance to try," said Dennis. "The teacher said it was time to get ready for dismissal and that I could try to balance the sword tomorrow. So I came home and made a sword like Jane's to practice with."

Einstein picked up the sword. It had been made

from a long, straight piece of wood. One end had been cut down to make it come to a point. The other end had been wrapped with many layers of foil until it was quite heavy. A smaller piece of wood had been taped at right angles just below the foil to form a hilt.

"Have you been able to balance the sword for two minutes?" Einstein asked.

"No," admitted Dennis. "I can't make it stay up for more than ten or fifteen seconds. After that it begins to fall to one side or the other."

"Let's see you try," Einstein said.

"O.K." Dennis held his hand away from his body and placed the hilt of the sword on two fingers. Then he moved his hand back and forth slightly as he tried to keep it from falling over. After a few seconds the sword began to waver back and forth. Dennis tried to move his hand but could not prevent the sword from falling to the floor.

"I think I'm going to lose my baseball cards," Dennis said sadly.

"Not necessarily," Einstein said. "I can show you one trick that will make balancing the sword much easier."

Can you solve the puzzle: What trick will help Dennis balance the sword and win the bet?

"That would be great!" Dennis exclaimed. "What should I do?"

"Try balancing the sword with the point, not the hilt, resting on your fingers," Einstein said.

"That's crazy, Einstein," Dennis said. "The hilt is much heavier than the rest of the sword. How am I supposed to balance the sword with the heavy part so high up?"

"Just try it," urged Einstein.

Dennis placed the point of the sword on his fingers. Even though the sword wavered back and forth, he was able to move his hand in time to keep the sword from falling down.

"Wow! It works," Dennis said happily. "But I don't understand why."

"You can keep anything from falling over if you support it under its center of gravity," Einstein said. "The center of gravity in the sword is in the hilt, where most of the weight is concentrated."

"But why can't I balance it with the hilt on my fingers?" Dennis asked.

"Because then the center of gravity is very low, just above your fingers. When it begins to wobble, it has just a short distance to fall. That doesn't give you much time to move your hand. That makes balancing very difficult."

"What happens when I try to balance the sword on its tip?" Dennis asked.

"Then the center of gravity is high up, far away from your fingers. It takes much more time to fall. That gives you enough time to move your fingers back under the center of gravity and makes it easier to keep the sword from falling. Try balancing a broom on your hand. It's much easier when the heavy part is high up."

"I suppose Chuck will demand that I give him half the baseball cards when I win the bet," Dennis said. "What a friend!"

Einstein laughed. "Chuck seems to be the kind of friend that's hard to find," he said, "and even harder to lose."

6

Fireside Story

"Dad, did you hear about the rooster that refused to fight?" Einstein asked his father.

"You mean because he was chicken?" Dr. Anderson responded.

"Did I tell you that joke before?"

"No," said Dr. Anderson. "Your grandfather told it to me about thirty years ago."

"Did he also tell you why dragons sleep during the day?" persisted Einstein.

"I don't remember. Why do they?"

"So they can fight knights," Einstein said. "And did you hear about—"

"Adam, please," Dr. Anderson laughingly interrupted, "you're working in my office today to straighten out the files, not to tell me jokes."

"Sure, Dad. Whatever you say. As the first person to use the bathtub each day, you're the ringleader."

"Adam!"

"I'm going, going, gone." Einstein hurriedly left his father's examination room and went into the outer office, where the files were kept. Einstein said hello to Miss Holden, the receptionist, and then set to work filing records.

Dr. Anderson was a veterinarian who worked in an animal hospital. Einstein worked at the hospital after school every Tuesday and Thursday. He helped with the animals and also did clerical jobs.

After working on the files for a few minutes, Einstein heard the front door open. He turned to look at the person who came in. It was Mr. Evans, a man who had recently worked at the hospital for a short time. Einstein recalled that Evans had been dismissed last week for some reason or other.

"Oh, it's you, Evans," Miss Holden said with no enthusiasm. "What are you doing here? You've been paid all your salary."

"That's not why I'm here," Evans growled. "I left a pair of my shoes up in the storeroom, and I'm just going to go up there and get them."

"Maybe I should ask Dr. Anderson," Miss Holden said, but Evans brushed past her desk and went up the stairs.

"Mr. Evans seems angry about something," Einstein said.

"He always seems angry," Miss Holden replied. "I never liked him very much. I didn't like the way he treated the animals. He always seemed to hurt them more than was just accidental. I think Dr. Anderson felt the same way."

"I wonder if getting his shoes was the real reason he came back," Einstein said.

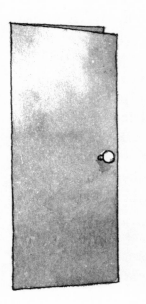

Just then Dr. Anderson ran out of his office.

"I smell smoke!" he exclaimed. "Adam, run out-side and look around the building. Miss Holden, call the fire department and ring the alarm bell and get everyone in the building down here. I'm going upstairs to check the rooms on the second floor."

Einstein ran outside and looked up at the hospi-tal. At first he didn't see anything unusual, but then he noticed thin wisps of smoke coming out of an attic window.

Einstein ran back inside. "There's smoke coming out of the attic!" he exclaimed.

Some of the hospital staff grabbed fire extinguishers and ran up the stairs. Einstein was about to get an extinguisher and follow when he noticed Evans calmly walking down the stairs. It's odd that Evans is so calm while everybody else is so excited, thought Einstein. Also, where are the shoes he said he was going to get?

"Excuse me, Mr. Evans," Einstein said. "Did you see how the fire got started?"

"What do you mean by that?" Evans demanded angrily. "Are you saying I started the fire?"

"No, but the fire is in the storeroom in the attic. And that's where you said you were going."

Evans was silent for a moment. Then he said, "Yeah, the fire started up there. But it was an accident."

Dr. Anderson came down the stairs with a fire extinguisher in his hands. "Just how did the fire start, Evans?" he asked. "We managed to put out the fire. But we were lucky. If we hadn't spotted it so soon, who knows what might have happened?"

"It was an accident," Evans repeated.

"You were going to tell us how the fire started," Dr. Anderson said.

"Yeah. It was like this. I was looking for my shoes in the storeroom but the bulb was broken and it was very dark up there. I lit a match to look

around. I was holding up the match and it touched
one of those big dusty cobwebs that are all over the
attic. In a second the cobweb burst into flame. The
burning cobweb must have set fire to the other
webs and then to the room."

"That can't be true," Einstein said.

Can you solve the puzzle: How does Einstein
know that Evans is lying?

"Are you calling me a liar?" Evans demanded. "That's what happened, and you can't prove otherwise."

"I think I can," Einstein said quietly. "You just said that the flame of the match touched a cobweb and it started to burn and set off other webs."

"That's what happened," Evans declared. "The cobweb started to burn so quickly that there was nothing I could do."

"That's not true," Einstein said. "Cobwebs don't flame—they just char and then go out quickly. So the webs couldn't have started the fire. You must have started the fire deliberately."

"Get out of here now, Evans," Dr. Anderson said angrily. "And if I ever see your face around here again, I'll call the police."

When Evans had left the hospital, Dr. Anderson turned to his son. "Einstein," he said, "that was a wonderful bit of science. I didn't know you were interested in spider webs."

"Spiders are very interesting," Einstein said. "In fact, Evans' story reminds me of the name you give to spiders when they're first married."

"What name?"

"Newly *webs*," Einstein replied.

7
The Weather Balloon

Ms. Taylor was talking to Einstein's class before they were due to board the school bus. Ms. Taylor was Einstein's science teacher. She was taking the class on an outing to the weather station at State University.

"We're fortunate that we're scheduled to visit the weather center today," Ms. Taylor said. "They're planning to launch a number of weather balloons, and we should be in time to see some of them."

"I bet I could hit one of those balloons with a rock and knock it down," Pat whispered to his friend Herman, who was standing beside him.

Ms. Taylor stopped speaking and stared at Pat. "Pat Burns, I can't believe what I just heard," she said. "We will be guests at State University, and we must behave ourselves. Any nonsense on your part will be severely punished. Do I make myself clear?"

"Yeah," Pat said. "I was only kidding."

"But I bet you could knock it down," said Herman.

"Herman believes everything Pat tells him," Einstein remarked to Margaret. "It saves him from thinking."

Herman glared at Einstein. "Who asked you?" he said. "Pat can't give me any help when it comes to brains. Right, Pat?"

Pat groaned. "Forget it, Herman," he said.

"Let's quiet down and listen," Ms. Taylor said. "We'll get to State University about eleven o'clock and eat our lunches at the athletic field there. We may see some balloons in the sky about that time. After lunch we'll come back to the bus at twelve o'clock and go to the center, where we'll be given a tour."

When the bus arrived at the athletic field, the children in the class quickly scattered. Some started to eat right away, but Einstein and Margaret decided to have a catch with a Frisbee before they sat down to eat.

"Did you hear that King Kong caught a flying saucer and was playing with it," Einstein said. "He thought it was a Frisbee."

Margaret held her nose. "That's awful," she said. "But I think King Kong would rather travel by flying saucer than by flying carpet."

"Why?" Einstein asked warily.

"Because traveling by flying carpet is too *rugged*. Get it?"

"Speaking of carpets, what did the rug say to the floor?"

"What?"

" 'Don't move. I've got you covered.' "

Margaret groaned and said, "I'll stop if you will."

"Agreed," said Einstein. "And as the cannibal said, 'Let's go and find some friends for lunch.' "

"Einstein!" Margaret exclaimed. "But that's a good idea. Let's find Sally and Mike and eat lunch with them."

Einstein and Margaret started to walk over to a grassy spot where a number of their classmates were sitting. But just as they were about to sit down, it began to rain. Einstein and Margaret grabbed their lunches and ran to take cover under a clump of trees at the edge of the field. When they reached the trees, they saw Pat and Herman holding a downed weather balloon.

"Did you knock down that balloon?" Margaret asked. "That was really stupid. How could you do it even after you were warned?"

"We didn't knock it down!" Pat exclaimed. "It just started to come down a few seconds ago. Herman and me were just sitting here having lunch. When we saw the balloon coming down, we grabbed hold of it."

"Do you expect anyone to believe that story? And here comes Ms. Taylor now," Margaret said.

"I want everyone to get back to the bus," Ms. Taylor said. Suddenly she saw the balloon and stopped. "Oh, no," she said. "You really knocked down a balloon, didn't you, Pat?"

"No, we didn't," Pat said. "We just now saw it sinking to the ground, so we went over to get it. That's the truth."

"We'll see about that, young man," Ms. Taylor said angrily. "You and your friend Herman just can't be trusted."

"Excuse me, Ms. Taylor," Einstein interrupted. "But I don't think Pat and Herman did knock down the weather balloon."

Can you solve the puzzle: Why does Einstein think that Pat and Herman are not responsible for the weather balloon's coming down?

"You can't expect me to believe that a very light-weight helium-filled balloon is just going to sink to the ground by itself," Ms. Taylor said.

"Not by itself," Einstein said. "But not by anything that Pat or Herman did. First of all, it's unlikely that anyone could hit a weather balloon with a rock. It's much too high. Also the mylar or neoprene material of the balloon would have to tear to let the helium out. And that balloon is still inflated."

"Then why did the balloon sink to the ground?" Margaret asked.

"I think it was because of the rain," Einstein said. "It started to rain just a few minutes ago. The water stuck to the balloon and made it just heavy enough to start to sink. Pat and Herman were telling the truth when they said they ran over to a downed balloon."

"So that's why the balloon came down," Pat said.

"Right," said Einstein. "Can you imagine what would have happened to the balloon if it had rained cats and dogs?"

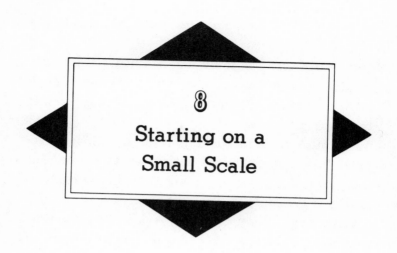

8

Starting on a
Small Scale

The phone rang just as Einstein was sitting down after dinner to watch a movie on TV. The movie was an old science fiction film called *Them*. It featured a nest of giant ants that liked people—as a snack.

"Hello," Einstein said, picking up the phone.

"I'm afraid there's something wrong with my new invention," Stanley said without bothering to say hello. "Can you come right over?"

"Can't it wait?" asked Einstein. "I'm just sitting down to watch a movie about giant ants. *You* should enjoy watching the film. Remember how you nearly sent for some just-hatched giant ants?"

"How can you watch that stuff?" Stanley asked. "You're the one who proved to me that giant ants can't exist."

"Because it's fun making believe," Einstein replied. "Anyway, what did you invent this time? Let me guess. You invented a large monkey wrench so that gorillas can get a grip on things."

"Not very funny," Stanley said. "If you come over now, I'll let you try out another invention of mine. It's a new type of glass cleaner. You can clean your eyeglasses with it and they'll stay clean for as long as a month."

"Is that the same cleaner you told me about last week? You used it to clean the windows in your house and it turned black in the sunlight. It took you days to scrape it off the windows."

"Well, I made a slight mistake with the formula," Stanley admitted. "But I corrected the error." He paused. "I think."

Einstein sighed. "I suppose I can come over after school tomorrow. But you have to promise me you won't make me use your glass cleaner."

"O.K." Stanley agreed reluctantly. "I'll see you tomorrow."

After school the next day Einstein walked slowly over to Stanley's house. Along the way he used a magnifying lens to watch a tiny jumping spider. The little hunter was small and quick. It had eight eyes in its head, which gave it good vision. It could jump many times its own length.

Einstein also spotted a common garter snake moving through the grass. He knew it was a garter snake because of the three yellow stripes running the length of its body. Of course, Einstein made no attempt to catch or injure the snake. He had often read about how important snakes are in keeping the balance of nature.

By the time Einstein arrived at Stanley's house, Stanley was not in a very good mood.

"Late as usual," Stanley said.

"Sorry," said Einstein. "I was watching the world's snappiest snake—a garter snake."

"Forget those silly jokes," Stanley said. "This is serious. Come upstairs to my laboratory and I'll show you."

Stanley's "laboratory" was in its usual messy state. A space had been cleared in the center of the room for a weird-looking contraption.

"This is my newest invention," Stanley said proudly. "It's a scale."

"I can't *weight* to see how it works," Einstein said.

"The scale is super-accurate," Stanley said, ignoring Einstein's pun. "It will tell your weight to the nearest fraction of an ounce or gram."

"Then what's wrong with it?" Einstein asked.

"The problem is that I can't seem to make the pointer stay on one spot. Even when I stand perfectly still on the scale, the reading keeps changing slightly." Stanley pushed back his long black hair. "I can't figure out what's wrong."

"Let me weigh myself and see," Einstein said.

Einstein stepped on the scale. Sure enough, no matter how still Einstein stood, the pointer kept moving slightly up and down.

Einstein pushed back his glasses and thought for a minute. "Stanley," he said, "this time your invention isn't at fault, so take heart. There's another reason the pointer keeps varying."

Can you solve the puzzle: Why does Stanley's scale have the shakes?

"The reason that the pointer keeps bouncing has to do with your heart," Einstein said. "Or rather, with your heart and your blood. You know that your heart keeps filling and emptying with blood as it pumps."

"Everybody knows that," Stanley said impatiently. "But what does that have to do with my scale?"

"As the blood is pumped up and down in your body, your center of gravity keeps shifting. Your center of gravity is where all your weight is concentrated. As your weight keeps shifting up and down, the pointer of your scale keeps varying."

"So all scales will have the same shakes," Stanley said slowly.

"Right," Einstein said. "For a one-hundred-pound person, the movement is a little greater than half an ounce."

"Then if I put a rock or some other object on my scale, the needle will be still?" Stanley asked.

"That's so," Einstein agreed. "You know, a scale is like a road map—they both show the *weigh*."

"Want to try my glass cleaner?" asked Stanley.

9

The Rain in Sparta

Sparta Middle School was going to present the musical *My Fair Lady* tomorrow at its annual spring performance. The play was to be performed under a large tent set up at Big Lake State Park. All the tickets had been sold. The proceeds were to be used to buy needed supplies for the school.

Mrs. Michaels, Margaret's mother, who was a professional singer, had volunteered to direct the performance.

"There are only two things to worry about now," she remarked to Margaret and Einstein. "The first is that Pat remembers not to knock over the scenery when he is onstage in the ballroom scene. The second is that the show tent doesn't leak. It's been raining every day this week."

"I hope the tent is waterproof," Margaret said. "The audience will be sitting on the grass or on blankets. I can just imagine what will happen if the ground is wet. Maybe we should go up to Big Lake and make sure the tent hasn't leaked."

"That's a good idea," Mrs. Michaels said. "Why don't we drive up and stop on the way for dinner? Would you like to come with us, Einstein?"

"Sure." Einstein agreed. "I'll phone home and tell my parents I'll be back late."

The drive up to Big Lake State Park took about an hour. Einstein and Margaret played Twenty Questions to pass the time. Margaret nearly stumped Einstein with a mineral that began with the letter "E." Finally Einstein guessed that it was element number 99, einsteinium. Margaret said that he should be ashamed of himself for taking so long to guess. For once Einstein couldn't think of a comeback.

It was still raining when they arrived at the State Park. Mrs. Michaels parked her car near the large tent, and they all got out.

Einstein looked down at the wet grass and shook his head. "As the ground said to the rain, if you

keep this up, my name will be mud," he joked.

"That's too true to be funny," said Mrs. Michaels. "We'd better take a look inside the tent."

They walked over to the tent and opened one of the flaps. It was dark inside, but in an instant they knew the worst. The bright green grass inside the tent looked lovely, but it was soaking wet. No one would be able to sit on the ground.

"How could this have happened?" Mrs. Michaels asked. "We paid the Big Top Tent Company and told them to set up the tent two weeks ago. The tent doesn't seem to be leaking, but the ground is soaked."

"I've got an idea," Margaret said. "We can call the tent company and ask them to cover the ground with a canvas. Maybe they can even set up benches or chairs for people to sit on."

"We can ask them, Margaret, but it will probably cost a lot of money to get them to come out again," Mrs. Michaels said gloomily.

"I think you should call them," Einstein said thoughtfully. "I wonder if they can explain how the grass got so wet under the tent."

"O.K., let's call them," Mrs. Michaels agreed.

There was a phone booth in the administration building near the lake. In a few minutes Mrs. Michaels was talking to the owner of the tent company, Mr. Hoover.

"The grass is all wet under the tent, and we need a canvas cover for the ground," she said. There was a pause, and then she said, "No, that's too expensive. We can't afford to pay you that much. I just don't know what to do."

"May I speak to Mr. Hoover?" asked Einstein.

"Here's the phone, but I don't think it will do any good."

"Mr. Hoover, this is Adam Anderson talking. Could you tell us why the ground got so wet under the tent? You were supposed to set up the tent two weeks ago. That was before the rains began."

"Listen, kid," growled Mr. Hoover, "the tent was set up two weeks ago on time. I suppose some water must have gotten in under the flaps or something."

"I think you just set up the tent a few days ago, Mr. Hoover," Einstein said. "And that makes *you* responsible for the grass being too wet for us to perform the play."

"Prove it," said Mr. Hoover.

Can you solve the puzzle: How can Einstein prove that Mr. Hoover did not set up the tent two weeks earlier, before the rains began?

"The tent couldn't have been up for two weeks," Einstein said. "The grass is bright green."

"What does that prove?" asked Mr. Hoover. "Grass usually is green."

"Not grass that has been inside a dark tent for two weeks," Einstein explained. "The chlorophyll in grass needs sunlight to stay green. After two weeks without sunlight the grass would look brown and faded. Not bright green."

"Yeah, well—er—er—maybe I could see my way to putting some canvas on the ground without charging any more money."

"Do you think you could also put in some folding

chairs?" Einstein asked innocently. "It's for a good cause."

"I suppose so," grumbled Mr. Hoover. "Anything else?"

"That would be just fine. And why don't you come to the play as our guest?"

Einstein hung up and turned to tell Mrs. Michaels and Margaret what had happened. Then he said, "I wonder if I should tell Mr. Hoover the best way to pitch a tent?"

"What's the best way?" asked Mrs. Michaels.

"Sometimes overhand and sometimes underhand," said Einstein. "It depends on how far you want to pitch it."

"That joke is strike three," said Margaret.

10
The Big Parade

Einstein wasn't very happy. Margaret had been chosen to be the grand marshal of the annual school parade. She was going to ride at the head of the parade in the royal sedan chair. That part was O.K. But Margaret had chosen Einstein as one of her four escorts and chair bearers. And Einstein didn't care much for that.

"Carrying a sedan chair is hard work," grumbled Einstein when Margaret asked him. "You need a person with a strong back and a weak mind. Why me?"

"Which of those qualifications is missing?" Margaret laughed. "Seriously, though, it was an honor to be chosen grand marshal. And you're the first one I thought of to be my escort. But if you'd rather not, I'll pick someone else."

Einstein pushed back his glasses and thought for a moment. Then he said, "You have to choose four sixth graders as escorts. How about choosing Mike, Pat, and Herman along with me?"

"I'll be happy to choose you and Mike, but why Pat and Herman? Oh, wait a minute. I get it. Strong backs and weak minds. Well, they certainly qualify. Anyway, I'm happy you decided to be one of my escorts."

"With you sitting in the sedan chair, I guess I can *bear* it," Einstein said.

"I'll give that pun three hearty *chairs*," Margaret countered.

Parade Day was sunny and warm. The route of the parade led from the school yard through the downtown area of Sparta. Then it circled back and finished at the Sparta High School athletic field, a distance of about one mile.

When Einstein arrived at the starting point, Mike was standing by the sedan chair. The sedan chair was simply a gold-painted wooden chair with two long aluminum poles attached to the sides. It was decorated with paper streamers and had a sign that

said, "Grand Marshal." Even with Margaret sitting in the chair, the whole contraption weighed less than a hundred pounds.

"This thing shouldn't be too difficult to carry," Mike said to Einstein. "I can lift the chair by myself. And with four of us carrying Margaret, each of us will be carrying only one-fourth the weight. It's just carrying the chair for a mile that worries me."

Einstein smiled. "It may be easier than you think," he said mysteriously. "When Pat and Herman get here, I want you to go along with anything I say to them."

Before Mike had a chance to reply, Pat and Herman arrived.

"Hello, weaklings," Pat said to Einstein and Mike.

"When Pat says 'Hello,' he tells you all he knows," Einstein observed.

"Yeah? Well, another thing I know is that Herman and me are the strongest kids in the class," Pat said. "We'll see who gets more tired carrying the chair."

"I'm sure Margaret chose you because she has a great deal of respect for your strength, Pat," Einstein said. "You know, it's really an honor to be an escort for the grand marshal. The closer you get to the grand marshal, the more honored you are."

Pat looked suspiciously at Einstein. "I guess you're right," he said. "Margaret must really like me."

"Oh, she does, Pat," Einstein said. "In fact, it would be an honor if we carried the chair like this." Einstein leaned close and whispered something to Pat.

"If you say so, Einstein," Pat said. "It's fine with me."

Margaret came over to the chair. She was dressed in the imperial robes of the grand marshal (actually some bed sheets). "Are all my escorts ready?" she asked.

"Load up and let's move out," Pat said.

Margaret sat down in the chair and arranged her robes. "I'm ready," she announced.

Pat and Herman went to the front of the chair and Einstein and Mike went to the back. Each of the boys grasped a pole and lifted the chair together. Then each boy placed the pole on his shoulder and they all began to walk in step.

The parade took less than an hour. When they arrived at the high school athletic field, Pat and Herman looked tired and sweaty. But Einstein and Mike were fresh and happy. Pat couldn't figure out what had happened.

Can you solve the puzzle: What had Einstein suggested to Pat that resulted in Pat and Herman's doing most of the work?

Later that day Einstein explained to Margaret what had happened.

"Pat believes any great thing anyone says about him," said Einstein. "I told Pat that you chose him because he was so strong. Then I suggested that it would be a great honor if he walked closer to the grand marshal than Mike and me."

"I noticed that," Margaret said. "But what difference did that make?"

"The closer Pat was to the chair, the harder it was for him to carry it," Einstein said.

"Why?" asked Margaret. "There were four of you carrying the chair. Each of you should have been carrying only one-fourth the weight."

"That would be true if each of us were the same distance from the chair. You see, carrying the chair is like balancing a seesaw. A fifty-pound person can balance a hundred-pound person if he sits twice as far from the center. Mike and I were four feet from the chair. Pat and Herman were only two feet from the chair. So they did twice as much work as we did."

"Did you figure that out all by yourself?" Margaret asked admiringly.

"Actually, Archimedes discovered the principle more than two thousand years ago," Einstein said modestly.

"It serves Pat right for being such a hotshot," Margaret said.

"True," said Einstein. "Pat is always blowing his own horn. But that's because he's always in such a big fog!"

ABOUT THE AUTHOR

SEYMOUR SIMON is one of America's leading science writers for young readers. Mr. Simon has written more than sixty books, among which are *The Secret Clocks, Look to the Night Sky, The Paper Airplane Book*, and *Pets in a Jar*, all published by Viking.

For many years Mr. Simon was a science teacher in junior high school. He lives on Long Island.